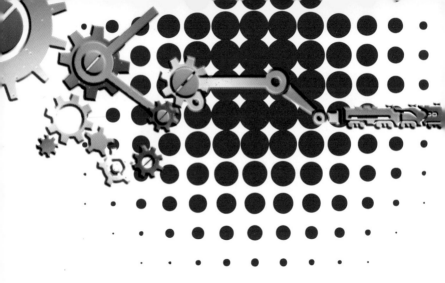

First published by Parragon in 2012

Parragon
Queen Street House
4 Queen Street
Bath BA1 1HE, UK
www.parragon.com

ISBN 978-1-4454-9710-5

Printed in China

LIGHTS, CAMERA,
ACTION CHUGGER

Based on the episode "Lights, Camera, Action Chugger",
written by Sarah Ball.

Bath • New York • Singapore • Hong Kong • Cologne • Delhi
Melbourne • Amsterdam • Johannesburg • Shenzhen

Emery had an exciting job for the day. He was going to be helping out on the set of Action Chugger's new movie. **"Honking horns!"** Brewster gasped. He had always wanted to rub wheels with the stars, but today he was on litter picking duty with Calley.

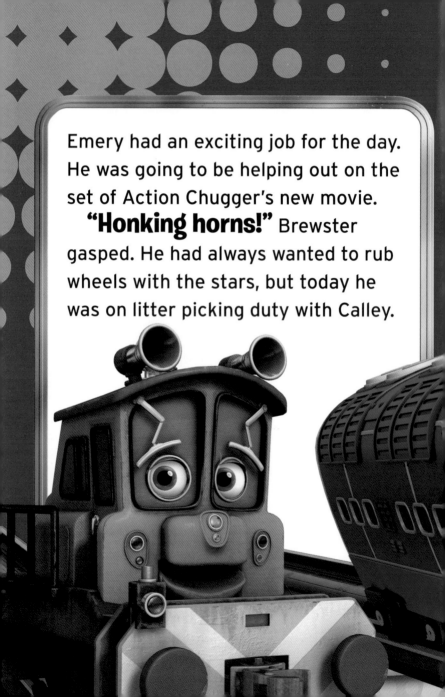

Brewster thought litter picking would be boring, but Calley showed him that it could be fun.

"This wagon can do some pretty nifty things," she said, swinging the magnet picker arm like a lasso to catch a tin can.

"That was incredible," gasped Brewster. "Can you teach me?"

"Absotootly!" replied Calley.

"Prepare to be amazed!" Brewster called as he swung the magnet arm. His throw was a little too strong and the wire whirled wildly before clamping onto Calley's horn. **Clunk!**

"It's alright," Calley chuckled. "You just need to practise. I'll see you back at the depot," she called, chugging away to find more litter.

Emery was working his wheels around the film set, trying to be as helpful as possible, but he kept getting his bumpers in the way. There was a lot of waiting around and he found it hard to be quiet.

"This chugger is ready to movie-it along!" Emery called eagerly.

Meanwhile, the star of the film was missing. Action Chugger was nowhere to be seen! Where was that super chugger?

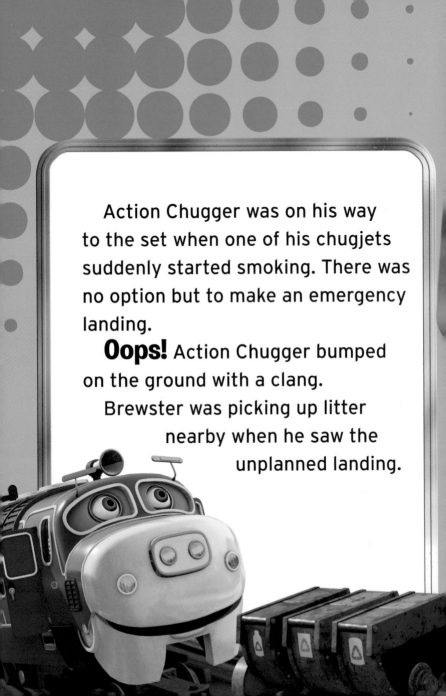

Action Chugger was on his way to the set when one of his chugjets suddenly started smoking. There was no option but to make an emergency landing.

Oops! Action Chugger bumped on the ground with a clang.

Brewster was picking up litter nearby when he saw the unplanned landing.

"Honking horns!"

At first, Brewster thought it was a movie stunt, but then he realised that Action Chugger was in a spot of trouble.

"Brewster to the rescue!" he shouted, chugging to his hero's side.

"My systems have shut down," Action Chugger told Brewster. **"Can you get me back on my wheels?"**

Brewster had a clever idea and zipped into position. Carefully, he swung his litter picker arm around, just like he had with Calley. The magnet landed very close to Action Chugger's clamp, so Brewster tried again and this time the magnet caught it.

"Good work citizen!" Action Chugger called.

Brewster was bursting with pride as he slowly pulled his hero upright.

"One, two, three, pull!"

"Chugtastic! Now you're my hero," cheered Action Chugger. **Wow!** Brewster couldn't wait to tell Koko, Wilson and Emery that he had impressed Action Chugger!

Brewster noticed that a tree branch had got stuck in Action Chugger's chugjet.

"That's what must have caused you to lose power," he said, pulling it out.

"Supersonic!"

Soon Action Chugger was firing on all cylinders. He asked Brewster if he wanted to come and watch the film shoot.

"Honking horns! Do I ever!" Brewster gasped.

Action Chugger buckled up to Brewster, then took him soaring high into the air. They were going to fly to the movie set! Brewster couldn't believe his luck.

When they landed on the film set, Action Chugger introduced Brewster as his special guest.

"Lights, camera...Action Chugger!" Brewster shouted through the director's megaphone. Wilson, Koko and Emery watched in amazement.

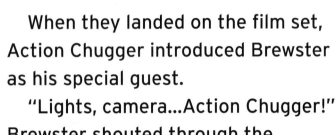

"Lights, camera... Action Chugger!"

"Wowzer!" Wilson gasped as Action Chugger rolled and whizzed through the air, thundering across the sky with chugjets blasting, climbing higher and higher.

Brewster beamed as Action Chugger banked to the side and whooshed back to them, straight towards the set.

"Traintastic!" Koko called.

What an amazing day it had turned out to be!